MR. NOISY
and the Giant

Roger Hargreaves

D0767424

Original concept by
Roger Hargreaves

Written and illustrated by
Adam Hargreaves

Mr Noisy is the noisiest person you will ever meet.

His voice is so loud it can shake the birds from the trees.

It can even shake the birds from the trees across the other side of the world!

Last month, Mr Noisy decided to call his friend
Mr Quiet, who lives many, many hills away.

But Mr Noisy does not have a telephone. He does
not need one.

Do you know what he does when he wants to speak
to someone?

He goes out of his front door and shouts!

When Mr Quiet heard Mr Noisy's booming voice,
he nearly jumped out of his chair.

Mr Noisy's loud voice scares most people.

When Mr Jelly met Mr Noisy, he was so frightened that he ran straight home and stayed under his bed for a week.

And when Mr Noisy said hello to Little Miss Splendid, he made her hair stand on end.

But Mr Noisy is not the only person with a huge voice.

There is one other person who is just as loud as Mr Noisy.

That person is a Giant.

A Giant who lives surprisingly close to where you live, but even closer to Mr Noisy.

The Giant is enormous.

His feet are the size of sofas.

He is so tall that he has to bend down to look into Mr Tall's bedroom window.

But by far the biggest thing about the Giant is his voice.

And that is the Giant's biggest problem in life.

Whenever he tries to talk to anyone, they run away.

His huge, loud, booming, thunderous voice terrifies everybody.

Just one **"HELLO!"** is enough to send them running for the hills.

And so the Giant is a very sad and lonely Giant.

One hot summer's day, the Giant was resting on the river bank, cooling his feet in the water, when he heard footsteps.

Very loud, thumping footsteps.

And the very loud, thumping footsteps were accompanied by whistling.

Whistling as loudly as a train whistle.

The Giant was very excited.

That must be another Giant, he thought to himself.

Another Giant who could be my friend.

The Giant peered over the hill. But on the other side of the hill, he did not see another Giant.

I am sure you can guess who he saw instead.

That's right!

It was Mr Noisy!

"HELLO!" boomed the Giant, in his quietest voice.

But because Mr Noisy is so used to loud noises he did not run away like anyone else would have.

"HELLO!" he boomed back, in a voice as loud as the Giant's.

In no time at all, the Giant and Mr Noisy were chatting.

The loudest chat in the world!

The Giant so enjoyed their chat that he invited Mr Noisy to tea.

And to the Giant's delight, Mr Noisy accepted his invitation.

The Giant talked and talked and talked, while Mr Noisy sat sipping tea out of the Giant's thimble.

They talked right through the afternoon and into the evening.

They talked so late that Mr Noisy was invited to stay the night.

In the Giant's extraordinarily large spare room.

In the Giant's extraordinarily large spare bed.

The two of them snored so loudly that they very nearly shook the roof off the house!

The next morning, while having a swim in the Giant's extraordinarily large bath, Mr Noisy had an idea.

He explained his idea to the Giant over breakfast.

"I HAVE A FRIEND CALLED MR QUIET," boomed Mr Noisy, **"AND HE USED TO LIVE IN A PLACE CALLED LOUDLAND. I THINK THAT YOU AND I SHOULD GO ON HOLIDAY TO LOUDLAND!"**

"WHAT A GREAT IDEA!" thundered the Giant.

And so off they went.

And it was perfect.

Because, you see, in Loudland everything and everybody is loud.

Extremely loud.

Even the worms are loud in Loudland.

Mr Noisy and the Giant could be as loud as they liked.

They fitted in very well.

Except for one thing.

One very LARGE thing.

The Giant could not fit into his hotel bed!